HANGOUT HANG-UPS!

A wave of shoplifting has hit the Bear Country Mall, and everyone is a suspect—especially the cubs! With no place left to hang out, what are Brother, Sister, and the rest of the gang to do? Will their new music teacher help them find a place to go after school? And can she really give them the key to unmasking the thieves?

BIG CHAPTER BOOKS

The Berenstain Bears
AT THE TEEN ROCK CAFE

by the Berenstains

A BIG CHAPTER BOOK™

Random House 🏠 New York

Copyright © 1996 by Berenstain Enterprises, Inc.

http://www.randomhouse.com/

Library of Congress Cataloging-in-Publication Data
Berenstain, Stan.
The Berenstain bears at the Teen Rock Cafe /
by Stan and Jan Berenstain.
  p. cm. — (A big chapter book)
SUMMARY: When recent acts of shoplifting at the mall make store owners suspicious of the bear cubs who hang out there, the cubs decide to find out who the real shoplifters are.
ISBN 0-679-87570-0 (pbk.) — ISBN 0-679-97570-5 (lib. bdg.)
[1. Shoplifting—Fiction. 2. Shopping malls—Fiction.
3. Bears—Fiction.] I. Berenstain, Jan. II. Title.
III. Series: Berenstain, Stan. Big chapter book.
PZ7.B4483Bemie   1996
[Fic]—dc20   96-1854

Printed in the United States of America   10 9 8 7 6 5 4 3 2

Contents

Chapter 1
Where There's Smoke,
There's Fire...

It was the first day of winter term at Bear Country School. The schoolyard was lightly dusted with frost as the cubs gathered to wait for the morning bell.

The first day of a term is a new beginning. And whenever you have a new beginning, you're sure to hear rumors about what to expect. As the cubs chatted and gossiped, and clapped their mittens together to keep their hands warm, a rumor about a new teacher was going around the schoolyard.

Now, rumors are slippery things. They have a funny way of getting all stretched and bent out of shape as they spread. And this rumor was no exception.

"New teach today," Skuzz said to Too-Tall. "Pass it on, boss."

Too-Tall caught Queenie McBear's eye and gestured for her to come over. Their on-again, off-again thing was off again this

week, and he thought that passing on a juicy rumor to her might be just the spark that could get them together again.

"Big news, sweetcakes," he said. "New teacher today. Pass it on."

Queenie's eyes got wide. "Really? Who?"

Too-Tall shrugged.

Queenie frowned. "Well, is it a he or a she?"

Too-Tall just shrugged again. At that, Queenie put her hands on her hips and glared at him. "Some rumor-passer-on *you* are," she said. "I hope you can at least tell me who this new teacher is replacing."

Too-Tall didn't want to disappoint Queenie. So he leaned over and whispered in her ear, "I can't vouch for this, but I heard it might be...er, uh...Teacher Bob."

Queenie let out a gasp. *"Teacher Bob?* You're *kidding!"*

With a smug smile, Too-Tall folded his arms across his chest and shook his head.

"You're *not* kidding!" cried Queenie. "This isn't big news. It's *huge!* Thanks, big guy!"

Queenie hurried over to a group of cubs that included Brother and Sister Bear, Lizzy and Barry Bruin, Babs Bruno, Cousin Fred, Bonnie Brown, and Ferdy Factual. "Totally awesome news, guys," she said, her eyes sparkling with excitement. "Teacher Bob's leaving!"

The cubs were shocked. No one spoke.

"How can that be?" said Lizzy finally. "I just saw him looking out of his classroom window."

"Isn't it obvious?" said Queenie. "He came to say good-bye and introduce the new teacher."

"Oh, no," said Bonnie. "This is awful!"

"Now hold on," said Brother. "It's only a rumor. A rumor can be like a puff of smoke—here one minute, gone the next."

"I'm not so sure about that," said Babs. "You know what they say: Where there's smoke, there's fire."

"Smoke?" said Barry, looking around. "I don't see any smoke."

Chapter 2
The Announcement

Teacher Bob was one of the most popular teachers at Bear Country School. The cubs were all abuzz about the rumor as they filed into his classroom. The buzzing continued even as he stepped to the lectern and announced, "There will be a special assembly first thing this morning to introduce a new teacher."

Instantly the class fell silent. It was so

quiet you could have heard a pencil drop. In fact, a pencil did drop—Cousin Fred's. The sound it made hitting the floor seemed like a cannon shot.

"Then it's true!" Queenie blurted out. "You're leaving!"

Teacher Bob turned to Queenie with a puzzled look. "Leaving? Me?" He smiled. "I'm not leaving. But Miss Acappella, the choir teacher, is. Just for a term, to study music at Big Bear University. That's why we're having the special assembly. So Mr. Honeycomb can introduce her replacement."

The whole class breathed a huge sigh of relief. Queenie seemed to shrink in her seat. Her face turned tomato red.

"Queenie the Rumor Queen," muttered Harry McGill in the back row, just loud enough for everyone to hear.

The whole class roared with laughter. Queenie turned around to stare daggers at Too-Tall, who pretended not to notice.

Meanwhile, Ferdy Factual leaned forward and snickered at Babs Bruno in the row ahead of him. "Where there's smoke, there's fire, you say?" he whispered. "Well, *I* say: Where you think there's fire, sometimes there's just a lot of *hot air*."

"You think you're so smart!" snapped Babs.

"Well, I do have a name to live up to," said Ferdy. "And it's Ferdy *Factual*, not Ferdy *Rumor*."

"Yeah, but don't forget you've got a nickname, too!" said Babs. *"Nerdy Ferdy!"*

Teacher Bob clapped his hands loudly. "That's enough, Babs and Ferdy," he said. "Quiet down, everyone." He glanced at his watch. "It's time for assembly."

Chapter 3
New Teacher

The assembly audience grew quiet as the school principal, Mr. Honeycomb, stepped to the podium. All eyes were fixed on the only other bear on the stage. She sat on a folding chair behind Mr. Honeycomb. She was dressed quite strangely for a school assembly, in a long black gown and a lovely pearl necklace. Beside her stood a shiny grand piano.

"Good morning, cubs and teachers," said Mr. Honeycomb. "I suppose you all know by now that our regular choir teacher, Miss Acappella, will be away this term studying at Big Bear University. I am pleased to say that we have someone *from* Big Bear University to take her place. This term our choir will be led by the talented musician seated behind me. Let me introduce Ms. Arpeggio."

Now, the cubs had always loved Miss Acappella. She was relaxed and full of smiles. She never had a nasty word for anyone, no matter how badly they sang.

But Ms. Arpeggio seemed different. She sat ramrod straight in her chair, looking straight ahead with a grim expression on her face. She didn't move a muscle—not even to smile—when Mr. Honeycomb said her name.

In the audience, Cousin Fred said to Brother, "Uh-oh. I think our choir is in for a change."

"Yeah," said Brother. "A change *for the worse*."

"Why is she all dressed up like that?" Sis-

ter whispered to Lizzy Bruin. "She can't be going to a dinner party. It's only eight in the morning."

"I'll bet she's going to play the piano," said Lizzy. "That's how they dress to play that classical stuff. Like Ludwig van Bearthoven."

"But Miss Acappella never gets all dressed up to play the piano," said Sister.

"If *you* hit as many clunkers as Miss Acappella," said Lizzy, "would *you* get all dressed up to play the piano?"

"Guess not," said Sister.

"Instead of making a speech," continued Mr. Honeycomb, "Ms. Arpeggio has decided to introduce herself by playing the piano for us. By the way, she has offered to give free piano lessons after school in the music room on Wednesdays and Fridays. And now, without further ado, Ms. Arpeggio will play her very own piano version of the famous 'Trout Quintet' by Franz Schubear."

Ms. Arpeggio walked to the piano and seated herself. She stared straight ahead. There was no expression on her face. The auditorium went dark except for a few lights shining down on her. A hush fell over the audience as she placed her fingers on the keys.

Suddenly, the vast room was filled with sound. Beautiful sound. Never before had the cubs of Bear Country School heard so many notes and chords come out of a piano

all at once. At times Ms. Arpeggio's hands moved so quickly they seemed a blur. And yet, in all those racing, streaming notes, not a single one was off tune or out of place. It was truly amazing.

After a few minutes the piece was over.

As Ms. Arpeggio sat with her fingers still pressing the keys, the last notes echoed through the auditorium and died away. The cubs and teachers sat stunned.

Ms. Arpeggio rose, turned to the audience, and bowed deeply. But still she didn't smile. Everyone clapped. The applause grew louder as Ms. Arpeggio bowed once more and walked stiffly into the wings. And that was that. Although the applause went on for some time, she did not return.

The cubs filed through the halls to their classrooms. Brother Bear, walking with Bonnie Brown, was lost in thought. Finally, he turned to Bonnie with a little smile and said, "So, if Ms. Arpeggio challenged Miss Acappella to a piano-playing contest, who would win?"

Bonnie laughed. "I know you're joking," she said. "But let me tell you, I think Ms. Arpeggio would win even if you tied her hands behind her back and made her play with her *feet*."

"You play the piano, don't you?" said Brother. "Are you going to take lessons from Ms. Arpeggio?"

"No way," said Bonnie. "I'd be embarrassed. She's not just good—she's *too* good. And I hate to think what choir practice is going to be like from now on. You can kiss those nice relaxed rehearsals good-bye."

"So, when's the first practice?" asked Brother uneasily.

Bonnie gave him a doomed look. "Tomorrow afternoon."

Chapter 4
Mall Mayhem

After school that day, Brother and Sister and their friends got together at Bear Country Mall.

There were several spots around town where the cubs liked to hang out. Sometimes they went to the Burger Bear or Biff Bruin's Pharmacy. But their favorite hangout these days was the mall.

The Bear Country Mall was a huge building filled with stores and walkways. What

the cubs liked best about it was the freedom it gave them. They didn't have to stay put in a booth or squeeze into the narrow aisles of a single store. They could stroll up and down the wide walkways and go into any store they liked. And when they got tired of walking and spending their allowances, they could sit along the edge of the big fountain across from Jeans R Us and flip pennies into the water.

"What did you wish for?" Brother asked Bonnie, who had just tossed a penny into the fountain.

"If I tell you, it won't come true," Bonnie said.

"Aw, come on," said Brother.

"Oh, I guess it's all right," said Bonnie. "It won't come true anyway. I wished that Miss Acappella would come back to school in time for choir practice tomorrow afternoon."

"You just wasted a perfectly good wish," said Barry Bruin. "But I sure know where you're coming from."

"Well, *I* think Ms. Arpeggio is really cool," said Babs Bruno.

"She's cool, all right," said Barry. "She's so cool, she's *frozen*. Did anyone see her smile?"

The cubs all shook their heads.

"I don't think we should give up on Ms. Arpeggio just because she's a serious musician," said Ferdy Factual in his typical bored tone of voice.

"Oh, you don't?" said Bonnie. "And how long do you think Ms. Arpeggio, with her long black gown and her pearls and her perfect piano playing, will put up with all the mistakes we make in choir practice? I see that as a problem. Don't you?"

Ferdy yawned. "I prefer to see it as a challenge."

"Okay, Ferdy," said Harry. "And when you hit a wrong note in choir and Ms. Arpeggio gives you that icy stare, then you can feel *really* challenged."

Bonnie put the back of her hand to her forehead and gazed off into the distance, as if she were acting in a play by Shakesbear. "Methinks our lovely days of relaxing choir practice are over," she said. "Please, dear Miss Acappella, come back… oh, please…please…*please*…."

The cubs laughed.

Brother chuckled and looked at the fountain, bubbling and splashing away peacefully. "Well," he said, "at least we still have a nice relaxing after-school hangout."

Just then a security guard came up and stared hard at the cubs. He made sure they all noticed him staring at them before he walked on.

"Guess I spoke too soon," said Brother. "The mall sure isn't what it used to be."

The mall had indeed been a tense place lately. During the last few weeks there had been a lot of shoplifting. Nearly all the stores had been hit. The Bears Roebuck department store had lost thousands of dollars in merchandise.

The thieves were clever. In fact, Police Chief Bruno had been unable to catch them. Meanwhile, the owners, managers, and clerks of the mall shops were growing more and more suspicious of their customers. They had even hired extra security guards to patrol the mall.

Another security guard wandered by, then circled around and came up to the cubs. He was a great big powerful bear. On his uniform was a name tag that said B. BIGGS. (The "B." stood for "Burly.")

"What're you cubs up to?" said Burly Biggs in a nasty tone of voice.

"We're just hangin' out," said Brother Bear.

"Yeah," said Queenie. "You don't have to look at us like we're a bunch of criminals."

"Chill out, Queenie," said Brother. "Let me handle this."

Just then a shout was heard from inside Jeans R Us. Out ran the manager, Mr. Denham. He hurried over and grabbed the security guard's arm. "We've been robbed!" he yelled. "A dozen pairs of jeans! That's the third time this month!" He looked fiercely at the cubs.

The cubs had spent some time in Jeans R Us before resting at the fountain. Babs had even bought a pair of jeans.

Burly Biggs pointed at Babs's Jeans R Us shopping bag. "Do you have a receipt for those jeans, cub?" he demanded to know.

Babs looked shocked. "Do you think I *stole* them?" she gasped. *"Me*, the *police chief's daughter?"*

"I don't care who you are," snarled the guard. "I want to see a receipt!"

Babs dug out her receipt and showed it to him.

"Hmm," he said, reading it. "Okay." He turned to Harry McGill. "You hiding anything behind that wheelchair, son?"

Harry couldn't help laughing. "You've gotta be kidding!" he said.

"This is no laughing matter!" barked the guard. "Open up those coats and jackets, all of you!"

As Burly Biggs searched the cubs for stolen jeans, Mr. Denham looked up and down the mall. "Which way did your friends go?" he growled at the cubs.

"Friends? What friends?" said Brother.

"Those rowdies who came into my store with you."

"You mean the Too-Tall gang?" said Brother. "They came in *after* us, not *with* us."

"Yeah, and they left *before* you," said the manager. He turned to the security guard. "Nice little racket they're running. These cubs come in and buy one pair of jeans while their friends are stealing a dozen."

"*What?*" cried Sister Bear. "We're not running any racket!"

"I'll have you cubs arrested!" yelled the manager.

"Now calm down, Mr. Denham," said the security guard. "There's nothing we can do.

I'LL HAVE YOU CUBS ARRESTED!

We have no evidence on these cubs."

"You're darn right you've got no evidence!" said Queenie. "You've also got no *manners!*"

"Don't you talk to me like that!" cried Mr. Denham.

"You cubs better move along," said the guard.

"Why?" said Cousin Fred. "We haven't done anything wrong."

"Just move along," said the guard. "Go on down to the other end of the mall."

The security guard put his big, burly arm around the manager's shoulders and tried to calm him down. They walked back toward the store.

"This is ridiculous," muttered Brother as the cubs trudged off down the mall.

"Yeah," said Bonnie. "I'd rather be in choir practice with Ms. Arpeggio!"

Chapter 5
A Shaky Start

The cubs didn't have to wait long to find out what choir would be like. The very next afternoon they gathered in the auditorium.

"Where's Ms. Arpeggio?" asked Lizzy.

"Probably wants to make a grand entrance," said Queenie.

Babs noticed a stack of sheet music sitting on the edge of the stage. She went up to take a look. "It's 'Ode to Joy' by Ludwig van Bearthoven," she said.

"Oh, great," said Harry. "Classical. I'll bet it's impossible to sing."

Just then one of the side doors of the auditorium opened and in walked Ms.

Arpeggio. Babs dashed back to her chair.

Ms. Arpeggio stood in front of the stage, facing the cubs. She wasn't wearing her black gown and pearls. She had on an ordinary blouse and skirt. But the cubs hardly noticed the change. What they did notice was her height. When they had seen her on the stage the day before, the cubs hadn't realized she was even taller than Mr. Honeycomb. Now, as she towered above them, they were more afraid of her than ever.

"Welcome to choir practice," she said. "I want you to form two rows in front of the stage, shorter cubs in front and taller cubs in back." She pointed to Bonnie Brown. "You may pass out the music."

Soon the cubs were ready. They clutched their sheet music as they stared up at their new teacher.

"All right," said Ms. Arpeggio. "First,

each of you tell me your name, then sing the first three bars of 'Ode to Joy.' We'll start with the front row and go from left to right." She nodded at Sister, who was at the left end of the front row. "You may begin."

Sister peered up at Ms. Arpeggio over the edge of her sheet music. "Do you mean alone?" she asked in a small voice. "I have to sing...*all alone?*"

"That's right," said Ms. Arpeggio. "I want to find out how high your singing voices are and how well you can sight-read music."

Sister gulped. "Sister B-B-Bear," she said in an even smaller, squeakier voice. Her knees started to shake. She tried to hold the music steady. It didn't really look so hard. In fact, it looked pretty easy. But she was so nervous, she wasn't sure she could get a single note out.

Sister took a deep breath and sang the

first note. But what came out of her mouth wasn't a musical note at all. It was more like the sound a cat makes when you step on its tail.

The other cubs couldn't help giggling. Barry Bruin even laughed out loud.

All of a sudden the cubs were silent. Ms. Arpeggio was giving Barry her icy stare. Sister held her breath as the teacher's piercing eyes moved along the rows of cubs until they were looking straight at...*her.*

It was a moment before Sister realized that the icy stare was gone. In its place was a warm smile. Slowly, Sister let out the breath she'd been holding.

"That's all right, Sister," said Ms. Arpeggio gently. "You may try again when you're ready. But before you do, I think we'd all better relax for a minute. You must realize, I've never led a cub choir before. Only grown-up choirs. So I hope you'll be patient with me."

The cubs looked at each other. Had they heard right? Had the fearsome Ms. Arpeggio apologized to them? Had *she* asked *them* to be patient with *her?*

The rest of choir practice went smoothly. Once the cubs relaxed, they sang loud and clear. And by the end of the hour, "Ode to Joy" was ringing out across the auditorium as though the cubs had been practicing it all term.

"Wonderful!" cried Ms. Arpeggio as the bell rang to end the period. "Ludwig van Bearthoven would be proud of you all!"

Chapter 6
Hot on the Trail

"I couldn't believe it," said Brother.

"You could have knocked me over with a feather," said Bonnie.

"You could have knocked *me* over with *half* a feather!" said Sister.

The cubs were sitting beside the fountain at Bear Country Mall. All they could talk about was that afternoon's choir practice.

"Just goes to show you," said Cousin Fred. "You can't judge a book by its cover."

"You may not have noticed," said Babs, "but Ms. Arpeggio wasn't even wearing the same 'cover' today."

"You mean that long black witch's dress?" said Barry.

"It's not a *witch's* dress, silly," said Babs. "And I still think it's cool."

"Well, cool or not," said Cousin Fred, "she sure seemed a lot nicer today than yesterday."

"I wish I could say the same for the mall," said Brother, looking over at Jeans R Us. "Get a load of this."

The cubs all turned to look. Two faces peered at them from behind a life-size cardboard cutout of Beary Manilow in a pair of

stone-washed jeans. The faces belonged to Mr. Denham and Burly Biggs.

"Oh, great," said Queenie. "They're hot on the trail of us criminals again."

Inside Jeans R Us, the store manager tightened his grip on the security guard's arm. "They're looking this way!" he said. "They're checking out the store, I tell you. Planning another burglary. Pretty soon that rowdy gang will show up, and before you know it these other cubs will be in the store looking at jeans, asking questions, and taking up all my time. Meanwhile, the gang will slip in and rip me off again! But *this* time we'll catch 'em in the act!"

"I'm not so sure," said Burly. "The thieves have never hit the same store two days in a row."

"Then why are those cubs checking out my store like that?" asked Mr. Denham.

"Maybe they see us watching them?" said the guard.

"Nonsense. They're in on it. I know it, you know it, and Chief Bruno probably knows it, too. We just can't prove it yet. Now, you keep an eye on those cubs. And the minute any of 'em so much as breaks one little mall rule, kick 'em out and ban 'em from the mall for life. That way we'll solve this shoplifting problem without needing any proof!"

"Okay, Mr. Denham," said the guard. "Whatever you say."

Just then the Too-Tall gang appeared near the entrance at the other end of the mall.

"Don't look now, Mr. Denham," said the guard, "but here they come. Movin' mighty fast, too."

"Good heavens!" said the manager. "They

must all be track stars! No, wait. It's skate-boards! They're all on skateboards! And what's that horrible racket?"

"One of them has a boom box," said the guard.

"Aha!" cried Mr. Denham. "Skateboards! Boom box! They're breaking mall rules! Let's go get 'em!"

Chapter 7
Banned for Life?

By the time Burly Biggs and Mr. Denham reached the mall fountain, Too-Tall and his gang were already lounging on their skateboards and chatting with the other cubs.

Too-Tall was deep in conversation with Queenie when the security guard's huge shadow fell across him. He looked up into the big guard's stern face.

"Hi, Burly," he said. "What's up?"

"Well, well, well," said the guard. "What have we here? A boom box and four skateboards?"

"Wow," muttered Vinnie. "I didn't know Burly could count that high."

"I heard that!" snapped the guard.

"Chill out, Vinnie," said Too-Tall. "Burly used to work for my dad. Apologize to him."

"Sorry," said Vinnie, with a shrug.

"We'll get rid of the skateboards and the boom box, Burly," said Too-Tall. "We don't want to make trouble for you."

"Trouble for *me?*" said the guard. "It's no trouble for me, Too-Tall. 'Cause you and your gang are outta here!"

"Right, right," said Too-Tall. "We'll ditch the props. Come on, guys..."

"You don't understand!" shouted Mr. Denham. "You're outta here for good! *Forever!*"

"Let me handle this, Mr. Denham," said Burly. He turned back to Too-Tall. "You don't understand! You're outta here for good! *Forever!*"

"Hey, this mall has an echo!" said Smirk.

He flashed his famous smug smile at Mr. Denham.

"Wipe that smirk off your face, cub!" yelled Mr. Denham. "What Burly said couldn't have been said any better if I'd said it myself!"

"But you *did* say it yourself," cracked Skuzz.

The gang laughed. But Too-Tall held up a hand to quiet them. "Wait a minute, guys," he said. "I think they're serious about this."

"You bet we're serious!" said Mr. Denham.

Now Brother stood up and faced the store manager. "But that's not fair," he said. "They said they'd get rid of the skateboards. You can't ban them from the mall for one mistake."

"Oh, can't I?" growled the manager. "I've half a mind to ban the rest of you, too."

"Us?" said Brother. "What did *we* do?"

"You don't fool me one bit," said Mr. Denham. "I know you're all in on it together."

Brother just stared at Mr. Denham. He could feel anger building up inside him, so he didn't answer right away. He could see very well where this "discussion" was going, and he wasn't the kind of cub who liked to get into loud arguments with grownups.

But Sister had always been as hotheaded as Brother was cool and collected. And she had a lot to say right now.

"So *that's* what this is all about!" she cried, glaring up at Mr. Denham. "You're just trying to get rid of us because you think we're the shoplifters!"

"I don't *think*—I *know!*" said the angry store manager.

"Well, I don't think you know, either!" said Sister.

Just then Chief Bruno pushed his way through the crowd of shoppers that had collected around the fountain. "Someone called me about a disturbance," he said, "and this looks like it. What's the problem?"

"I demand that you arrest these cubs," said Mr. Denham.

The chief looked around at all the cubs. "Which ones?" he said.

"These skateboarders, for starters," said the manager.

"Arrest them for skateboarding in the

mall?" said Chief Bruno. "Isn't that a bit harsh?"

"They ripped off my store, too," said Mr. Denham.

"Just now? You caught them in the act?"

"Well, no," said the manager. "It was that burglary I reported yesterday. I didn't catch them in the act, but I know it was them."

Chief Bruno heaved a sigh and put his hands on his hips. "Do you realize," he said, "that this is the *fourth* time I've rushed out here to the mall this week because somebody was accused of shoplifting? And not *once* has there been any evidence. Now, I know this has been a frustrating month for you and the other store managers. But you've got to be patient. Whoever the shoplifters are, we'll catch them with the goods sooner or later. Now go on back to your store, please."

Grumbling, Mr. Denham went back to Jeans R Us. Burly Biggs followed.

"Okay, break it up," Chief Bruno told the crowd. "Show's over. Too-Tall, get those skateboards and that boom box out of here—pronto."

When the Too-Tall gang had gone, the chief turned to the other cubs. "I'm keeping an eye on those troublemakers," he said. "Mr. Denham might just be right about them."

"It isn't them, Daddy," said Babs suddenly. She had closed her eyes and was holding very still.

"What's wrong, honey?" said the chief.

"I...I don't know...I just had a really strange feeling," said Babs. "It's something I saw a while back...right here at the mall...something odd...it might have been the shoplifters....But I can't quite pull it out of my memory."

"Who were they? What did they look like?" said the chief.

"Sorry, Dad. It's gone."

"That's not much help, honey," said the chief. "But if it comes back to you, let me know right away. In the meantime, you cubs

could help the situation by using another hangout spot until we find out who these thieves are. You can see how jumpy all the store managers and security guards are."

"Where do you suggest we go?" asked Ferdy Factual.

"How about the Burger Bear?" said the chief.

"There's not enough to do there," said Queenie.

"I have a suggestion, at least for today," said a voice behind the cubs.

The cubs turned. It was Ms. Arpeggio. She had a Bears Roebuck shopping bag in her hand.

"Why don't you cubs hang out at my house for the rest of the afternoon," she said. "I'm sure we can find something interesting to do."

Chapter 8
Rockin' with Ms. Arpeggio

Chief Bruno thanked Ms. Arpeggio for her kindness, and Harry McGill phoned his mom to come pick him up in their special van. Then the rest of the cubs piled into Ms. Arpeggio's station wagon, and off they went.

The cubs were pleased that their new choir teacher wanted to help them find something to do. But they were a little worried about what it might turn out to be. What worried them most was that they might end up having an extra choir practice at Ms. Arpeggio's house. They had enjoyed

the earlier one. But they were hardly ready for another one yet.

As soon as the cubs saw Ms. Arpeggio's living room, they were sure that a second classical music session wasn't far off. In one corner stood a baby grand piano with sheet music lying open on it. On top of the piano sat a large bust of Ludwig van Bearthoven. On the mantel above the fireplace sat a bust of Johann Sebearstian Bach. The walls were covered with paintings of musical instruments and photographs of Ms. Arpeggio leading the Big Bear University Choir and playing the piano with the Big Bear Philharmonic.

Ms. Arpeggio served pretzels and juice. As the cubs snacked, they told her about what had been happening in the mall.

"Since you're new in town," said Brother, "you probably don't know that this shoplift-

ing has been going on for a whole month."

"Mr. Denham thinks the Too-Tall gang is doing it," said Cousin Fred. "And that *we're* helping them!"

"I think he and my dad are wrong about Too-Tall being behind it," said Babs. "But my dad *is* right about one thing: We do need a new after-school hangout."

"Well, I can't offer you my home every afternoon," said Ms. Arpeggio, "but I'll try to help you come up with something. In the meantime, let's have some music." She rose and went to the piano.

"Uh-oh," whispered Barry to Babs. "Ludwig van Bearthoven, here we come."

"What shall we sing?" asked Ms. Arpeggio brightly.

The cubs looked uneasily at one another. No one spoke.

" 'Ode to Joy'?" Cousin Fred finally said.

"Oh, you cubs must have had enough of that one today," said Ms. Arpeggio. "Let's try something else."

"But we don't know any other classical music," said Queenie.

"It doesn't have to be classical," said Ms. Arpeggio. "What are your favorite songs?"

"Mine is 'Rockin' and Rollin'' by Iron Honeybee," said Queenie. "But I'm sure you don't know that one. It's rock."

"*Hard* rock, I believe," said Ms. Arpeggio. Instantly, she began pounding out the popular new hit on the piano and singing at the top of her lungs.

The cubs were stunned.

"That was great!" said Harry when she had finished. "Can you do 'Rock Around the Block'?"

"An oldie but a goodie," said Ms. Arpeggio.

She played it perfectly. This time the cubs all sang along.

Over the next hour, Ms. Arpeggio and the cubs ran through a dozen rock and pop hits, old and new. They played and sang so loud that they shook the floor and made the pictures on the walls vibrate.

Afterward, Ms. Arpeggio went to the

kitchen to refill the pretzel baskets and pour more juice. The cubs were happy and relaxed. Even Ferdy Factual, who didn't know most of the songs they'd sung, had a smile on his face.

"That was awesome!" said Queenie when Ms. Arpeggio came back from the kitchen. "This is a lot more fun than hanging out at the mall."

"I'm sorry we can't do this more often," said the teacher. "We're being awfully loud, and the neighbors might get upset."

"Same with my neighbors," said Harry. "Not to mention my *parents*."

"Same here," said all the cubs.

"If we could just find a special place," said Brother. "One where the neighbors aren't close enough to be bothered by the noise…"

Everyone thought.

"The Big Bear Cafe," said Ms. Arpeggio suddenly.

The cubs looked at her. "The Big Bear Cafe?" they said.

"The students at Big Bear University run their own cafe," said Ms. Arpeggio. "They sell drinks and snacks and play music. Sometimes they have poetry readings. And two or three nights a week there's a floor show with all kinds of acts—bands, singers, comedians, even magicians."

Barry looked puzzled. "I don't think they'd let us in," he said. "Besides, it's too far away."

The other cubs snickered.

"I believe what Ms. Arpeggio is suggesting, Barry," said Ferdy, "is that *we* set up a cafe of our own."

"That's a great idea!" said Queenie. "I could get the Too-Tall band to play!"

"And I could organize poetry readings!" said Babs.

"And I could do my stand-up comedy routine!" said Barry.

"We'll have all kinds of music!" said Bonnie.

"But especially rock!" said Queenie. "We'll rock like teens!"

THAT'S IT! THE PERFECT NAME: <u>THE</u> <u>TEEN</u> <u>ROCK</u> <u>CAFE!</u>

"That's it!" said Harry. "The perfect name: *The Teen Rock Cafe!*"

Brother waved his hands in the air. "Hold your horses, guys," he said. "I'll admit a cafe is a good idea. But before we name it and plan the floor show, shouldn't we find a place for it?"

The cubs fell silent. They all thought hard.

"I have an idea," said Lizzy. "Maybe there's an old room we could use in the Bearsonian Institution."

The other cubs groaned.

"The Bearsonian is a place of *science*," said Ferdy. "It may have a Hall of Rocks, but I hardly think my Uncle Actual would approve of a Hall of Rock *Music*."

"Of course he wouldn't," said Bonnie. "But *my* uncle might have just the place for us."

All eyes turned to Bonnie. She explained that automatic teller machines had become so popular in Beartown that her uncle, Squire Grizzly, was about to close one of the local branches of his Great Grizzly National Bank. She wondered if he might donate the building to the cubs.

"I may be new in town," said Ms. Arpeggio, "but I've already heard all about Squire Grizzly's great generosity. I think you should have a talk with him about this, Bonnie. If you'd like, I'll go along with you. Maybe I can help explain why you cubs need the Teen Rock Cafe."

"Gee, thanks," said Bonnie. "That might help a lot."

"Now, it's getting close to dinnertime," said Ms. Arpeggio. "I can give most of you rides in my station wagon, but Harry will need his van. Better call home, Harry."

Chapter 9
Hypnotic Suggestion

As they waited for the McGill van to arrive, the cubs thanked Ms. Arpeggio for a wonderful afternoon.

"We had no idea you'd turn out to be so much fun," said Queenie.

Ms. Arpeggio smiled and said, "At choir practice I got the feeling you were all a bit scared of me."

"Well, when you played the piano in assembly," said Sister, "you seemed so... *serious*."

Ms. Arpeggio laughed. "Yes, I suppose I did," she said. "That's how I get when I play classical music. You see, I like to play from memory, without sheet music. I have to concentrate very hard so I can remember every single note. I even put myself into a kind of trance when I play. Not a deep one, of course. But it does help me remember the music more clearly."

"Really?" said Babs. "Do you think a trance could help bring back another kind of memory?"

"What kind of memory do you mean?" asked Ms. Arpeggio.

Babs told her about her memory of maybe seeing the shoplifters at the mall. "If I could just remember exactly who and what I saw," she said, "my dad could solve these crimes. Then everything at the mall could go back to normal."

HYPNOSIS! OF COURSE!

"Hmm," said Ms. Arpeggio. "You're not talking about sharpening a memory that's already pretty clear. You're talking about a vague, hazy memory—a memory of something you weren't paying close attention to when you saw it. The only thing I can think of that might help you is hypnosis. That puts you in a much deeper trance."

"Hypnosis! Of course!" said Lizzy. "I've seen that in movies about lost memories. And it always works."

"Well, it doesn't always work in real life," said Ms. Arpeggio. "Sometimes the memories that come out in hypnosis aren't memories at all. Sometimes they're just imaginary. But it might be worth a try."

"Could *you* hypnotize me?" asked Babs.

"Oh, no," said Ms. Arpeggio. "You'd need a specialist for that. Perhaps you should talk to Dr. Gert Grizzly about this."

Chapter 10
Full Speed Ahead

Plans for the Teen Rock Cafe moved ahead more rapidly than anyone had expected. Squire Grizzly not only donated the former bank to the cubs but even offered to put in a soda fountain, snack racks, tables and chairs, and sound and lighting equipment.

As soon as the store owners at the mall heard about the cafe, they offered to help out. After all, maybe the cafe would keep the cubs away from the mall!

The Music Cave donated a piano, a hundred CDs, and enough rock posters to cover

the walls. Grizzmaster Electronics donated a neon sign for the entrance. And Burgers 'n' Berries donated a month's worth of snacks, soda pop, and milk shakes.

The cubs put Bonnie Brown in charge of entertainment because of her experience in show business. In no time at all she had lined up acts for the grand opening. The band would be Too-Tall and the Gangsters. Bonnie herself would sing show tunes backed up by her special collection of soundtracks. And Barry Bruin would do his stand-up routine: he would stand up and tell bad jokes until he was booed off the stage.

Cousin Fred would run the sound and lighting equipment, with Trudy Brunowitz and Harry McGill as his assistants. Queenie would take care of the soda fountain, and Sister and Lizzy would help her. Babs Bruno would organize poetry readings once a month.

And what would Too-Tall and his gang be when they weren't playing in the band? You guessed it—*security guards*.

Chapter 11
Top Billing

With all of this going on, Brother and Bonnie somehow found time one day to go with Babs to talk with Dr. Gert Grizzly about hypnosis.

"Now, which one of you cubs is sick?" asked Dr. Gert, leaning way back in her big swivel chair.

"None of us," said Babs.

Dr. Gert's eyebrows raised. "What seems to be the problem, then?"

"I lost a memory," said Babs. "An important one."

"*Our* memories are fine," said Brother,

pointing to Bonnie and himself. "We just came along to give Babs moral support."

"I see," said Dr. Gert with a smile. "And just where did you lose this memory, Babs?"

"At the mall," said Babs. "I'm not exactly sure *where* at the mall. And I'm not exactly sure *what* I saw. But I think it's a clue to the big shoplifting mystery."

"Hmm," said Dr. Gert. "An interesting problem. How can *I* help?"

"Could you hypnotize her?" said Brother. "Ms. Arpeggio, our new choir teacher, says it might help the lost memory come back."

Dr. Gert shook her head. "A good suggestion, cubs. But I don't know anything about hypnosis."

"Do you know another doctor who does?" asked Bonnie.

"The only one in these parts," said Dr. Gert, "is the great psychiatrist Sigmund

THE ONLY ONE IN THESE PARTS IS THE GREAT PSYCHIATRIST SIGMUND BRUIN...

Bruin of Big Bear University. He's an expert on hypnosis. I'd be happy to give his office a call."

All three cubs nodded.

Dr. Gert got Dr. Bruin's secretary on the phone and explained the problem. Moments later she hung up and said, "Well,

Babs, you've got the next available appointment."

"When is it?" asked Babs eagerly.

"June," said Dr. Gert.

"June!" said the cubs all at once. "That's *six months* from now!"

"Sorry, cubs," said Dr. Gert with a shrug. "Sigmund Bruin is a very busy bear."

"Isn't there someone else who could hypnotize me?" asked Babs.

Dr. Gert thought. Finally, she shook her head and said, "Only Ralph Ripoff. When he was helping me raise money for the new hospital wing, he told me about a magic act he used to do in the circus years ago. He would hypnotize volunteers from the audience. But that was just fun and games. Finding lost memories is serious stuff. A hypnotist needs special training for that."

The cubs looked glum. But suddenly

Brother's eyes brightened. "What was Ralph's act like?" he asked.

Dr. Gert chuckled. "He got the volunteers to do crazy things. They would imitate dogs and chickens, or pretend they were someone else. Must have been pretty funny."

Brother turned to Bonnie. "That would be a great act for the floor show at the grand opening of the Teen Rock Cafe!"

Bonnie agreed. But Dr. Gert was quite sure that Ralph would want to be paid for his act.

"We could pay him from the money we make selling drinks and snacks!" said Brother. "Just this once, for the grand opening. Could you call Ralph right away, Dr. Gert? The grand opening is the day after tomorrow, right after school."

Dr. Gert picked up the phone and dialed

Ralph's houseboat. She heard ringing, then Ralph's voice saying, "Hello, this is Ralph Ripoff speaking. I can't come to the phone right now, but if you leave me a message after the beep, I'll get back to you. Unless, that is, you happen to be a certain bear who has the crazy idea that yours truly cheated him in a poker game last night. In *that* case, don't bother to leave a message,

'cause you're *wasting your time—*"

Suddenly, Ralph's speech was interrupted by his parrot screeching, "Sucker! Sucker! Sucker!" and Ralph yelling, "Shut up, you birdbrain!"

"Cut it out, Ralph," said the doctor. "This is Dr. Gert Grizzly, and you can't fool me with that phony recording."

"Er…uh…well, hello, Dr. Gert!" said Ralph. "What a pleasant surprise! What can I do for you?"

Dr. Gert told him what the cubs wanted.

"Dust off my old hypnosis act?" said Ralph. "Hmm. Perhaps I could also set up a little poker table in an out-of-the-way corner of the cafe—"

"No dice, Ralph," said Gert. "This cafe is on the up and up."

"…or maybe a shell game out in front, on the sidewalk, not actually *inside* the cafe…"

"Absolutely not," said the doctor. "But the cubs are willing to pay you for the act. Wouldn't you like to make some *honest* money for a change?"

"Hmm," said Ralph. "I'm not sure I want to dirty my hands with honest money…"

"Okay, Ralph, forget it," said Dr. Gert. She winked at the cubs. "So long—"

"Wait! Don't hang up!" cried Ralph. "On second thought, I can't see any real harm in making a few honest bucks—as long as it doesn't become a habit. But I demand top billing. And I'll need a rehearsal. It's been so many years since I've done the act, I'm not sure it'll work."

The cubs agreed to give Ralph top billing and rehearsal time, and the deal was made. They left Dr. Gert's office feeling that they had made the best of a disappointing visit.

Chapter 12
The Terrible
Meat-Eating Chicken

The next day, after school, the cubs gathered at the Teen Rock Cafe. The grand opening was just a day away. Everyone got right to work. They wiped off the tables, filled the soda fountain, and placed snacks in the snack racks. Meanwhile, Cousin Fred hooked up the sound equipment so Too-Tall and the Gangsters could let loose with their wailing electric guitars and crashing drums.

Minutes later, Ralph Ripoff hurried in and waved his cane in the air. The wailing and crashing stopped.

"Sorry to interrupt the noise—er, music," said Ralph. "But I've got a little poker game lined up, and I need to get this rehearsal moving. Now, I'll need some volunteers for my act. Who wants to be hypnotized?"

"Me!" said Sister. "I've always wanted to be a chicken."

"Who hasn't?" said Ralph. "Okay. Anyone else?"

No one spoke up.

"How about you, Ferdy," said Ralph. "You've always been a curious cub. And I

mean *interested,* not *peculiar*—heh heh."

Ferdy yawned. "Oh, all right," he said. "But I think you'll find me quite a challenge. Hypnosis works only on the weak-minded, you know."

"I gladly accept the challenge," said Ralph. "Anyone else?" He looked around the room. "Come now, isn't there anyone else *brave* enough to be hypnotized by the master?"

"How about you, boss?" said Skuzz to Too-Tall.

"Forget it," said Too-Tall. "That hypnosis stuff is a lot of bunk."

"If it's a lot of bunk," said Skuzz, "then what have you got to lose?"

"Yeah, boss," said Smirk. "I wanna see Ralph turn you into a chicken."

Just then Queenie whispered something into Vinnie's ear. Vinnie smiled and said, "No need for that, Smirk. 'Cause the boss is *already* chicken, right, gang?"

At that, the three gang members started flapping their elbows like chicken wings and going, "Bawk bawk bawk bawk!"

"I ain't chicken!" said Too-Tall. "I'll show you bums! Come on, Ralph. Try to put me under!"

Everyone gathered around as Ralph sat Too-Tall in a chair. Then Ralph took a gold watch and chain from his vest pocket and dangled it in front of Too-Tall's face. "Watch the watch, Too-Tall," he said, swinging it slowly back and forth.

Too-Tall's eyes followed the watch. Back and forth. Back and forth. Back and forth.

"You are getting sleepy," said Ralph in a soothing voice.

Too-Tall's eyes started to close.

"Ve-e-r-ry, ve-e-r-ry sleepy," said Ralph.

"Now I'm going to count to three. And when I get to three, you will be completely asleep and under my control. One... two...*three*."

Instantly Too-Tall's eyes closed and his head tilted to one side.

"Now listen very closely, Too-Tall," said Ralph. "The sun is shining. It's a beautiful day in the barnyard. You are a chicken. Repeat after me: *I am a chicken*."

"I am a chicken," mumbled Too-Tall.

The audience giggled.

"When I reach the count of three again," said Ralph, "you will open your eyes and you will still be a chicken. One... two...three."

Too-Tall's eyes popped open. He stood up, put his fists against his hips, and began strutting round and round the chair. All the time he was flapping his elbows and going, "Bawk! bawk! bawk!"

The cubs roared with laughter. Especially the rest of the gang.

Too-Tall bent at the waist and made pecking motions at the floor.

"I see we have a hungry chicken, cubs," said Ralph. "Better throw him some grain."

Laughing, the cubs made grain-tossing motions.

BAWK! BAWK! BAWK!

Suddenly, Too-Tall straightened up and looked Vinnie in the eye. "No grain," he said in a high-pitched squawk.

"What's that?" said Ralph.

"No grain," repeated Too-Tall.

"I see," said Ralph. "Then what *do* you want to eat?"

"Meat," said Too-Tall, still staring at Vinnie. He puffed out his chest.

"Hey, I don't like the way he's lookin' at me," said Vinnie. "Wake up, boss."

"I want meat!" squawked Too-Tall, eyes still fixed on Vinnie.

"Stop him, Ralph!" said Vinnie. "Snap him out of it!"

Ralph snapped his fingers at Too-Tall. "Wake up, Too-Tall! Wake up! Oh, dear! I've lost control of him!"

"I want meat!" Too-Tall squawked again. "I...want...a...VINNIEBURGER!"

And with that, he charged straight at Vinnie, flapping his elbows wildly and squawking at the top of his lungs.

Vinnie let out a shriek and dashed through the nearest exit.

Now it was Too-Tall's turn to laugh. He laughed until tears ran down his face. "And let that be a lesson to all of ya," he said. "*Nobody* calls me 'chicken'!"

Ralph chuckled and put out his hand for Too-Tall to shake. "Nicely done," he said. "Of course, I knew you were faking it as soon as you started talking. Ordinarily, my chickens don't talk."

"Thanks for playing along, Ralph," said Too-Tall.

"My pleasure," said Ralph. "I always enjoy a good practical joke. But you're out of the act. You may be a great gang leader, but you're a lousy hypnosis volunteer."

Chapter 13
Ferdy's Hero

Ferdy Factual was next to be hypnotized. He looked bored when Ralph started swinging the watch.

As his eyes followed the watch, Ferdy said, "I really think you're wasting your—"

And just like that, he was out cold. His eyes were closed tight. His head lolled against his left shoulder.

"Only the weak-minded, eh?" Ralph chuckled. "I didn't even have to count to *one!*"

"Maybe *he's* faking, too," said Trudy Brunowitz, Ferdy's girlfriend.

"We'll see about that," said Ralph. "I'm

going to try something a little different with Ferdy, because he is…uh…different.

"Now, Ferdy, there are certain bears you admire very much. And there must be one bear you admire above all others. At the

count of three, you will become that bear. One…two…three."

Ferdy opened his eyes and stood up. He yawned and folded his arms across his chest. He didn't seem any different. In fact, he seemed just like himself.

"My father is a paleontologist, and my mother is an archaeologist," he said. "When I was a baby, they took me on digs to the farthest reaches of Bear Country. I did not attend school until I moved to Beartown to stay with my uncle, Actual Factual, the famous scientist. But that didn't hold me back, because I'm a genius."

Some of the cubs laughed.

"Ha ha, very funny," said Queenie. "Okay, Ferdy, you can stop. We get the joke."

But Ferdy stared straight ahead and continued speaking. "My interests include astronomy, geology, chemistry, microbiology, and quantum physics, just to name a few. I have received the Bearsonian Institution's annual award for cub scientists three years running…"

"And you'll be runnin' again, with me chasin' ya, if ya don't clam up!" said Too-Tall.

"Hold on," said Ralph. He looked deeply into Ferdy's eyes. "I don't believe he's faking. No…in my professional opinion, Ferdy is truly hypnotized."

"But he's not doing what you told him to," said Lizzy.

"Sure he is," said Trudy with a smile.

"He's being the bear he admires above all others. *Himself!*"

Queenie groaned. "What an obnoxious nerd!"

"I think it's kind of cute," said Trudy.

Ralph ordered Ferdy to sit down. Then he put him back to sleep.

"Now, cubs," he said, "don't tell Ferdy what happened. I want him to repeat this remarkable performance in my act tomorrow. And I suggest that one of you bring a camcorder." He winked. "We're going to play a little trick on Ferdy. If it works now, it'll work tomorrow, too. Here goes."

Ralph took out his watch again and set it swinging in front of Ferdy. "When I snap my fingers you will wake up and remember nothing that has happened since you fell asleep."

At the snap of Ralph's fingers, Ferdy's

eyes opened. He took one look at the watch swinging back and forth in front of his nose and yawned. "I don't believe it's working, Ralph," he said.

The cubs couldn't help giggling.

Ralph put his watch back in his vest pocket. "It must be that strong mind of yours, Ferdy," he said. "And I'll tell you another thing. Nobody can say you have low self-esteem."

That got a big laugh from the cubs. Ferdy looked puzzled.

"I don't know why that should be funny," he said. "Self-esteem comes from accomplishments. And I am a very accomplished cub."

"How about giving me another shot at you tomorrow?" said Ralph.

Ferdy shrugged. "If you want to ruin your act," he said, "who am I to stop you?"

Chapter 14
Double Trance

Sister Bear was the next one to be hypnotized. She got her wish of becoming a chicken and put on quite a show. She bawked and scratched until Ralph told her she was a dog. At that, Sister got down on all fours and crawled over to Cousin Fred. She looked up at him, panting and wagging her backside.

"She's wagging her tail," said Brother as the cubs all laughed. "She must like you, Fred."

"Of course she does," said Lizzy. "She's not just any dog. She's Snuff, Fred's hound dog!"

Next Ralph took a red rubber ball out of his pocket and handed it to Cousin Fred. "Let's see if Snuff will fetch," he said.

Fred tossed the ball across the room and said, "Fetch, Snuff!" Sister scrambled over to the ball, picked it up in her mouth, and hurried back to Cousin Fred. The cubs roared with laughter.

"I think that's enough for now," said Ralph. "Sister will do fine for the act." He snapped his fingers.

Sister opened her eyes and looked around. She stood up. *"Umph! umph! erg!"* she said.

"Don't talk with your mouth full, Sis," cracked Brother.

Sister snatched the ball from her mouth and stared at it as the cubs roared again.

"Sister, you were truly marvelous," said Ralph. "Now, cubs, if you'll excuse me—"

"There they are!" said a voice in the audience.

"Huh?" said Ralph.

Everyone turned to look at the speaker. It was Babs. She was pointing to a poster on the wall and staring at it.

"There they are! The old ladies!" she said.

Barry Bruin squinted at the poster. "I don't see any old ladies," he said.

"Of course not," said Ralph, looking closely into Babs's eyes. "She's imagining them. She must have been accidentally hypnotized when I put Sister under!"

The cubs gasped.

"But she's not just imagining!" cried Brother. "She's *remembering!*" He quickly told Ralph all about Babs's lost memory.

"This is serious," said Ralph with a worried look. "I'd better snap her out of it."

"Why?" said Too-Tall. "Afraid of what we might find out?"

The cubs all fixed their gaze on Ralph.

"*What?*" said Ralph. "Do you think *I*... shoplifting...? I'm a *swindler,* not a *thief!*"

"Then keep her talking," said Brother, "so we can solve these crimes!"

The cubs pressed in close around Babs.

"All right, Babs," said Ralph. "Tell me where you are."

Babs kept staring at the wall. "At the mall," she said. "In the parking lot. My mom and I are walking to the car."

"And what do you see?" said Ralph.

"Two old ladies," said Babs.

"Who are they?"

"I don't know," said Babs. "I've never seen them before."

"Can you describe them?"

"They're wearing bonnets and long dresses. They're all hunched over. And they walk funny. They sort of…waddle."

Ralph sighed and looked at the cubs. "Don't sound like shoplifters to me," he said. "Walk funny? Why, my dear old

mother waddles, too. It's her arthritis."

"Ralph's right," said Cousin Fred. "I've seen those old ladies at the mall a lot lately. They're just ordinary shoppers."

Babs started talking again. "That's funny...they're getting into a pickup truck....Two old ladies who drive a pickup truck..."

Instantly, the cubs quieted down and listened carefully.

"Now they're in the cab of the truck," said Babs. "They're taking off their bonnets...and they're...*lighting up cigars!*"

The cubs gasped again.

"Those aren't ordinary shoppers!" cried Queenie.

"I'll bet they aren't even old ladies!" said Barry.

"They sound like a couple of crooks, if you ask me," said Ralph. "And as you all know, I'm an expert on crooks."

Brother hurried to the phone to call the police station and tell Chief Bruno what Babs had remembered. Meanwhile, Ralph brought Babs out of her trance and told her what she had said.

"Chief Bruno will be right over!" announced Brother.

Minutes later, the cubs heard the chief's squad car pull up outside. They poured out onto the sidewalk.

"Are the Bear Detectives here?" called Chief Bruno from the car.

"We're here," said Brother with a nod to Sister, Lizzy, and Cousin Fred.

"I'm making you deputies for the rest of the afternoon," said the chief. "We're staking out the mall. Come on, get in."

The four cubs hopped into the squad car. And off they went!

Chapter 15
All Points Alert!

The Bear Detectives had helped Chief Bruno solve other cases. But they had never helped solve one that meant so much to them.

"If we can catch these crooks, Chief, the mall will be safe again for hanging out," said Brother as the squad car glided along the highway toward Bear Country Mall.

"True enough," said the chief. "But don't get your hopes up too much. Babs might have imagined all that stuff about old ladies lighting up cigars in a pickup truck."

"If she did," said Cousin Fred, "then she's got a lot better imagination than anyone ever thought!"

Just then the police radio crackled. "Calling Chief Bruno, calling Chief Bruno," said a female voice. "This is Officer Marguerite. Come in, Chief. Over."

The chief picked up his transmitter. "This is Chief Bruno. Go ahead, Officer."

"Chief, the mall's been hit by the shoplifters again. Jeans R Us—second time this week. The manager says he can't understand it. No customers have been in the store so far this afternoon. Over."

"No customers?" said the chief. "Is he sure?"

"Yes, Chief," said Marguerite. "No one except for a couple of old ladies."

Chief Bruno looked at the cubs. The cubs looked back at the chief.

"Aha!" he cried. "They got greedy—and now *we've* got *them!*"

"How's that?" said Officer Marguerite.

"All points alert!" said the chief. "Radio the security guards at the mall and post them at all the mall exits. Tell them to be on the lookout for two old ladies in long dresses and bonnets. Then get on over to the mall. I'm almost there now. Over and out!"

Chapter 16
Partners in Crime

When Chief Bruno's squad car pulled into the Bear Country Mall parking lot, a security guard was already standing at the main entrance to the mall.

"At least they won't get out *this* way," said Brother.

"Uh-oh," said Sister. "Looks like they already have! Look over there!"

Sister pointed across the lot. Two old ladies in bonnets and long dresses were waddling toward a battered green pickup truck.

Chief Bruno drove over and stopped the car in between the truck and the old ladies. Quickly, he got out. The cubs followed.

"That your truck over there?" asked the chief.

The old ladies nodded. Both wore wire-rimmed glasses. Their bonnets covered their ears and foreheads.

"Been shopping, have you?" said the chief.

The ladies nodded again and pointed to their shopping bags. Chief Bruno walked up to them and looked hard at their faces.

"Those are mighty nice glasses," he said to one of them. "Mind letting me have a look at them?"

The old lady handed over the glasses. The chief peered through them. "Hmm," he said. "This looks like ordinary glass." He frowned. Then he sniffed at the glasses and looked up at the ladies again. "Have either of you ladies been smoking *cigars* lately?" he asked.

The old ladies glanced at each other and shook their heads.

Just then Officer Marguerite's squad car pulled up behind the ladies. Chief Bruno pulled his pistol from its holster and pointed it at them. He motioned the cubs to stand in a row to one side. Officer Marguerite moved to the other side and placed her hand on the handle of her pistol.

"I *thought* I recognized that face," said the chief to the lady whose glasses he was holding. "Both of you, take off those ridiculous bonnets!"

The hunched-over old ladies straightened up and scowled as they yanked off their bonnets. They were taller than Chief Bruno!

"The Bogg Brothers!" cried the cubs all at once.

"Maybe you should say, 'The Bogg *Sisters!*'" said Chief Bruno. "Hands up, you two! And no funny business! Officer Marguerite, look under their dresses."

One at a time, Officer Marguerite pulled the dresses up to the brothers' knees. Each brother had a large potato sack tied between his legs. The sacks bulged.

Officer Marguerite untied the sacks and dumped them out on the ground. "Quite a haul, Chief," she said. "Two hair dryers, five curling irons, ten cans of motor oil, twenty bars of bath soap, and a dozen pairs of jeans."

"Wow," said Sister. "No wonder they walked funny."

Suddenly, one of the brothers snarled at her, and Sister jumped back with a shriek.

"That's enough outta you two!" barked Chief Bruno. "Cuff 'em, Marguerite. Then take 'em back to the station and lock 'em up."

Chapter 17
Rockin' and Rollin'

By the end of the day, the Bogg Brothers had confessed to all the other shoplifting thefts at the mall over the last month. They told Chief Bruno that they had driven to Big Bear City once a week and sold the stolen goods at the side of the road out of the back of their truck.

The next morning, the start of school was delayed so the cubs could attend a special awards ceremony at the town hall. Mayor Honeypot gave Bear Country Crime Solver Medals not only to Babs Bruno and the Bear Detectives but also to Ms. Arpeggio for coming up with the idea of hypnotizing Babs. He also gave one to Ralph Ripoff for hypnotizing Babs—even though it was an accident.

Mr. Denham was there to speak for all the owners and managers of the mall stores. After apologizing to the cubs he had accused of shoplifting, he presented each of them with a gift certificate for a pair of jeans at Jeans R Us.

It was a morning of newfound harmony in Beartown—almost. As soon as Ralph got his award, he slipped out and set up his shell game on the front steps of the town hall. Fortunately, Officer Marguerite followed him outside and made him take it down just seconds before the crowd started to file out of the hall.

The awards ceremony was kind of boring for the cubs. It was full of long speeches

that went on and on. But the cubs sat smiling all the way through them, for they were thinking of the *real* celebration that would happen after their short school day—the grand opening of the Teen Rock Cafe. What perfect timing!

Within minutes of the final school bell,

the Teen Rock Cafe was packed with cubs. The only grownup there besides Ralph Ripoff was Ms. Arpeggio. Since the cafe had been her idea, she had been sent a special invitation. Soda pop flowed like water, and snacks flew off the racks.

Bonnie Brown opened the floor show.

Her show tunes were a big hit with the audience.

So was Ralph Ripoff's hypnosis act. Sister Bear squawked like a chicken and barked like a dog. The cubs roared with laughter at her imitation of Snuff fetching a red rubber ball. But they roared even louder at Ferdy Factual's imitation of the bear he admired above all others.

Cousin Fred made a video of Ferdy's amazing speech. The cubs laughed and hooted as Cousin Fred played it back for Ferdy. But Ferdy just yawned and said, "I don't see what's so funny about my performance. In fact, I think it's rather impressive."

I DON'T SEE WHAT'S SO FUNNY ABOUT MY PERFORMANCE. IN FACT, I THINK IT'S RATHER IMPRESSIVE.

"I don't believe it!" groaned Queenie. "He's so conceited, he isn't even embarrassed!"

Finally, the rock music and the dancing got under way. Too-Tall and the Gangsters were in top form. They played most of the new hit songs and some oldies, too.

After a short break, Too-Tall announced they would start the second set with the latest number-one hit, "Rockin' and Rollin' " by Iron Honeybee.

As the cubs crowded back onto the dance floor, they looked over at the band with surprise and delight. It looked as if Too-Tall and the Gangsters had taken on a new member, at least for the grand opening of the Teen Rock Cafe.

There at the piano, hands at the keyboard, sat none other than Ms. Arpeggio

in a pair of designer jeans and an Iron
Honeybee shirt.

Too-Tall gave the downbeat, and the
Teen Rock Cafe was jolted with the wailing
of electric guitars, the crashing of drums,
and the pounding of a piano—not to mention the sound of five very loud singing
voices.

And the happy cubs rocked till they
dropped.

Stan and Jan Berenstain began writing and illustrating books for children in the early 1960s, when their two young sons were beginning to read. That marked the start of the best-selling Berenstain Bears series. Now, with more than one hundred books in print, videos, television shows, and even Berenstain Bears attractions at major amusement parks, it's hard to tell where the Bears end and the Berenstains begin!

Stan and Jan make their home in Bucks County, Pennsylvania, near their sons—Leo, a writer, and Michael, an illustrator—who are helping them with Big Chapter Books stories and pictures. They plan on writing and illustrating many more books for children, especially for their four grand-children, who keep them well in touch with the kids of today.